BOOT
&
SHOE

Marla Frazee

Beach Lane Books

New York London Toronto Sydney New Delhi and Pasadena!

To Steve Malk, who likes cats more

BEACH LANE BOOKS
An imprint of Simon & Schuster
Children's Publishing Division
1230 Avenue of the Americas
New York, New York 10020
Copyright © 2012 by Marla Frazee
BEACH LANE BOOKS is a trademark of
Simon & Schuster, Inc.
For information about special
discounts for bulk purchases,
please contact Simon & Schuster
Special Sales at 1-866-506-1949 or
business@simonandschuster.com.
The Simon & Schuster Speakers
Bureau can bring authors
to your live event. For more
information or to book an event,
contact the Simon & Schuster
Speakers Bureau at 1-866-248-3049
or visit our website at
www.simonspeakers.com.
Book design by Marla Frazee and
Ann Bobco
The text for this book was hand-lettered
by Marla Frazee.
The illustrations for this book are rendered
in black Prismacolor pencil and gouache
on Speckletone Madero Beach 70lb text
weight paper.
Manufactured in China
0712 SCP
10 9 8 7 6 5 4 3 2
Library of Congress Cataloging-in-
Publication Data
Frazee, Marla.
Boot & Shoe / Marla Frazee.
—1st ed.
p. cm.
Summary: Boot and Shoe are dogs who live
in the same house, eat from the same bowl,
and sleep in the same bed, but happily
spend their days on separate porches, until
a squirrel causes some serious confusion.
ISBN 978-1-4424-2247-6 (hardcover)
ISBN 978-1-4424-5706-5 (eBook)
[1. Solitude—Fiction.
2. Dogs—Fiction.] I. Title.
PZ7.F866Bno 2012
[E]—dc23
2011035990

Boot and Shoe were born into the same litter, and now they live in the same house.

They eat
dinner out of
the same bowl.

They pee on
the same tree.

At night, they sleep in the same bed.

But Boot spends his days on the back porch,
because he's a back porch kind of dog.

And Shoe spends his days on the front porch,
because he's a front porch kind of dog.

This is exactly
perfect for
both of them.

Then one day,
for no apparent reason,

a squirrel started
some
trouble.

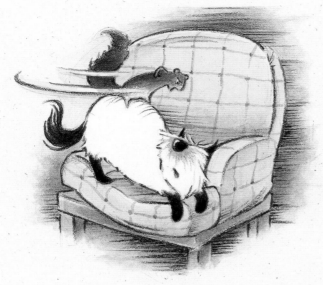

It chattered
at Boot.

It chattered
at Shoe.

It threw stuff
at Boot.

It threw stuff
at Shoe.

And then
it got all up
in Boot's business.

And it got
all up in
Shoe's business,
too.

Whoa.

Something had
to be done.

So Boot and Shoe
chased that squirrel
all over the place.

They chased it and
chased it and
chased it
until it
got
bored

and
walked
away.

Boot collapsed.

Shoe collapsed, too.

When Boot
   opened his eyes,
      he saw that he was on the front porch.
         He looked around for Shoe.
               Shoe should be here.
                     But he wasn't.

                           Oh, no.

When
   Shoe
opened his
   eyes, he saw that he was on the back porch.
      He looked around for Boot.
            Boot should be here.
                  But he wasn't.

                        Oh, no.

Boot searched
the front porch for Shoe.
He looked under things,
over things,
around things,
and between
things.

No luck.

Shoe searched
the back porch for Boot.
He looked under things,
over things,
around things,
and between
things.

No luck
for him
either.

Boot decided to station himself on the front porch
and wait there until Shoe found his way back.

And Shoe decided to station himself on the back porch and wait there until Boot found his way back.

It was
a long,
lonely
afternoon.

When it was dinnertime, Boot's stomach rumbled.
But he didn't want to eat dinner without Shoe.

Shoe's stomach rumbled, too.
But he didn't want to eat dinner without Boot.
It was a long,
hungry evening.

At bedtime, Boot was shivering.
But he didn't want to get in bed without Shoe.

Shoe was shivering, too.
But he didn't want to get in bed
                    without
                        Boot.

Once during the night,
Boot walked slowly around
to the back porch
to see if Shoe
was
there,

and Shoe
walked slowly
around to the front porch
to see if Boot was there.

But no luck again.

So Boot ended up back on the front porch waiting for Shoe,

and Shoe ended up back on the back porch waiting for Boot.

It was
a long,
sleepless
night.

The sun came up.

On the
front porch,
there was still no sign of Shoe.
Boot began to cry.

On the
back porch,
there was still no sign of Boot.
Shoe began to cry, too.

But, even in
the worst of times,
a dog still needs
to pee.

Boot dragged
himself over
to the tree.

Shoe dragged
himself over
to the tree,
too.

And suddenly, lo and behold, there they were again!

Overjoyed to see each other!

Overtired, too.

So even though the day was just beginning, Boot and Shoe decided

that the exact perfect thing for both of them to do was go right to bed.

Together!

(Of course.)